Quiet Wyatt Is A Riot!

By *Sherry Anne*

Illustrated By Chris Strange

Quiet Wyatt Is A Riot!

Published by
William Wyatt Publishing
Utica, NY
www.sherryanne.com

Printed in the United States of America

ISBN: 978-1-09830-959-6

This Book Dedicated To...

My sweet nephew William Wyatt,

From the time you were born, you brought adventure and laughter to the world. Believe in yourself. You can do whatever you put your mind to!

God bless you and keep you. (Num 6:24)

Love, Aunt Sherry

Quiet Wyatt is a riot...

full of
mischief –
and not
too quiet!

Quiet Wyatt is a riot...

he found a kite
– now watch him fly it.

Quiet Wyatt is a riot...

he eats an egg – see Daddy fry it?

Quiet Wyatt is a riot... he spills his milk – but Mommy dries it.

Quiet Wyatt is a riot...
he licks ice cream –

Quiet Wyatt is a riot...
he wants a toy –
will Grandma buy it?

Quiet Wyatt is a riot...
he hides a shoe –
does Grandpa spy it?

Quiet Wyatt is a riot...
he pulls a bow —

where Auntie tied it!

Quiet Wyatt is a riot...
he sees some paint –

Quiet Wyatt
is a riot...
he has a cat —
Oh no!
Don't dye it!

Quiet Wyatt is a riot...
full of mischief –
and not too quiet.

Quiet Wyatt is a riot...
he goes to sleep –
when the sky's twilit.

Quiet Wyatt... is finally... quiet.

Shhh...

About the Author

Sherry Anne was born with a bilateral hearing and speech impairment, yet achieved her Doctorate of Chiropractic degree and ran a successful practice for over 20 years. Now, she is a sought-after speaker and Gospel recording artist, having charted on Billboard's Music Video chart. Sherry Anne is an award-winning songwriter with many of her songs charting nationally. She has released six full length CDs, one children's CD, and a live DVD.

Sherry Anne has appeared in films and on television. She has authored two children's books: *How Are Ya, Arya?* and *Quiet Wyatt is a Riot!*; and is a contributing author for the book *Modern-Day Miracles*.

Sherry Anne loves to spend time by the ocean, and with her family and furry friends. She especially loves working with children and is dedicated to making a difference in the lives of others, offering hope, inspiration, and a powerful message of truth.

www.sherryanne.com